WELCOME TO

Beast Quest

Collect the special coins in this book.
You will earn one gold coin for
every chapter you read.

Once you have finished all the chapters,
find out what to do with your gold coins at
the back of the book.

With special thanks to Conrad Mason

For Elliot Cowle

www.beastquest.co.uk

ORCHARD BOOKS
Carmelite House
50 Victoria Embankment
London EC4Y 0DZ

A Paperback Original
First published in Great Britain in 2015

Beast Quest is a registered trademark of Beast Quest Limited
Series created by Beast Quest Limited, London

Text © Beast Quest Limited 2015
Cover and inside illustrations by Steve Sims
© Beast Quest Limited 2015

A CIP catalogue record for this book is available from
the British Library.

ISBN 978 1 40833 994 7

1 3 5 7 9 10 8 6 4 2

Printed and bound by CPI Group (UK) Ltd, Croydon, CR0 4YY

The paper and board used in this book are made from wood
from responsible sources.

Orchard Books
An imprint of Hachette Children's Group
Part of The Watts Publishing Group Limited
An Hachette UK company

www.hachette.co.uk

KANIS
THE SHADOW HOUND

BY ADAM BLADE

ORCHARD

CONTENTS

Greetings, followers of the Quest,

I am Irina, the Good Witch of Avantia's twin kingdom, Gwildor. This was supposed to be a time of happiness, as we welcomed young heroes Tom and Elenna to our capital city Jengtor. Freya, Tom's mother and Mistress of the Beasts, beamed with pride at the thought of her son's arrival.

She smiles no longer.

Someone else has been awaiting Tom's arrival. We should have known our enemies would choose this moment to strike. Now Freya lies in my chamber, unable to command her Beasts. And Jengtor is under siege from a deadly menace that attacks from the skies.

Our only hope lies with Tom and Elenna, but they are walking right into a trap.

Irina, loyal Witch of Gwildor

SNAKE EYES

Tom crouched next to Elenna,
hiding behind a cluster of barrels
on the deck of Sanpao's flying ship.
*Safe! Except now we're stuck
high up in the sky with a crew of
bloodthirsty pirates who might spot
us at any moment...*

Peering over the barrels, Tom
saw that the deck was bustling.

Sanpao's pirates were swarming up and down the rigging, swabbing the decks and adjusting the sails. They wore garish silks and satins, and clattered with weaponry – cutlasses, axes, clubs... Tom spotted the captain himself swinging in a hammock strung up between two masts, bellowing orders in between taking swigs from a flask.

"Stir your stumps, lads! Tie down those kegs, and look sharp about it!"

Tom felt a flicker of rage at the sight of his old enemy, with his greasy black ponytail, yellowing teeth and fading tattoos. Sanpao had done wicked things in the past, but this time he and the

witch Kensa had poisoned Tom's
own mother. And while Freya
lay sick in Jengtor, the capital of

Gwildor, Sanpao and Kensa were making plans to capture the city for themselves.

Tom gritted his teeth. *We're lucky the Good Witch Irina can protect Jengtor with her magic, because otherwise—*

"Look," whispered Elenna, interrupting Tom's thoughts. She was pointing to the far side of the deck. Tom followed her finger and saw their horses Angel and Star tied up.

Star spotted them and let out a hopeful whicker.

"Shh," Tom soothed the horse. Then with one swift movement he vaulted the barrels and crouched down behind a giant coil of rope. Elenna followed, landing softly next to him.

"There's something weird going on here," Elenna whispered.

"Is it the fact that we're on a flying pirate ship?" said Tom.

Elenna smiled. "Not that. It's the wind. Can you feel it?"

Tom licked his finger and raised it up high, but he couldn't feel a thing. He shook his head.

"Exactly," said Elenna. "But we're still going fast. And the sails are full."

Tom frowned as he studied the billowing sails. Elenna was right. *So what's powering the ship?*

He was about to look away

when his gaze fell on the base of
the mainmast. The wood seemed
to be shimmering with a purple
light seeping up from below the
decks. And there could only be one
explanation for that.

Magic!

"Sanpao's ship must be under some kind of spell," murmured Elenna.

"If we can stop the ship from getting to Jengtor, maybe we can save the city," said Tom. "I wonder how the magic works? Perhaps we could—"

"Look!" hissed Elenna. A giant man with an eyepatch was approaching their hiding place.

Tom glanced around and spotted an open hatch nearby. He grabbed Elenna's arm, darted across the deck and dived through the hatch, landing in a crouch on a wooden deck below. Elenna dropped down next to him. It was dark here, but a flickering glow of light spilled around the corner of a pile of crates. Tom edged closer, peering around the side of them.

Two pirates were sitting cross-legged around a lantern placed on the deck. One, a tall man with a long plaited beard, threw a pair of dice and groaned. "Gah! Snake eyes!"

The other chuckled. She was a wiry woman with a row of gold earrings. "Hard luck, mate. I'll win your share of the plunder before we even reach Jengtor!"

"Might be we never get there," grumbled the bearded pirate. "There's that magic shield round the city, remember?"

"Have a bit of faith, mate," said the pirate with the earrings, taking the dice. "Those cowards in Jengtor ain't the only ones with magic. Kensa has been burning a big hole right in the middle of the shield with her spells. We can fly straight through and take the city for ourselves!" She shook the dice. "And it ain't over then. I heard the cap'n and Kensa are going to build an army. After Gwildor, it'll be the Avantians' turn to taste our cutlasses." At last she rolled. "Ha! Pair o' fives!"

Tom and Elenna shared a glance. So that's what Kensa and Sanpao had been after, all along... They were planning to conquer not just

Gwildor, but Avantia too.

Well, not while there's blood in my veins!

"I still say it ain't goin' to be easy," said the bearded pirate, scooping up the dice. "What about Freya, that warrior woman?" Tom stiffened at the mention of his mother, Mistress of the Beasts here in Gwildor. "They say she can fight ten men at once, and command mighty Beasts into the bargain."

"I wouldn't worry about her," sneered his friend. "She's out cold thanks to Kensa's magic. Besides..." She leaned in closer, grinning nastily and tapping her nose. "Maybe you ain't heard, but we got an ally in

Jengtor. Someone on the inside. They'll make sure that no-good warrior never wakes up."

The bearded pirate rolled and groaned again.

"Ha ha! Ain't your day today!" cackled his friend.

The two of them froze as Sanpao bellowed from above. "Silvereye! Fleaspit! I'll give you to the count of five. If you ain't polishing the rollocks by then I'll keelhaul you myself!"

The two pirates scrambled to their feet so fast they knocked over the lantern. They hurried away, their faces white with fear.

As the light flickered and died, Tom's mind was working fast. *So Kensa and Sanpao have a spy inside Jengtor... But who could it be? Who would betray their own city?*

One thing was for sure. They had to find out fast, or Jengtor was doomed.

SABOTAGE!

"There's nothing for it," said Tom. "We'll have to take Sanpao hostage and force him to stop the ship. It's not going to be easy, though."

"You can say that again," Elenna replied with a sigh. "Let's start by getting out of this hold."

They crept round the edge of the crates. Tom noticed that, even

without the lantern, they weren't
in total darkness. On the far side of
the hold a soft purple glow lit up a
cluster of barrels.

Wait – purple... The same purple
colour he had seen earlier, at the
base of Sanpao's mast. Tom crossed
the lower deck.

"Where are you going?" Elenna
asked, but Tom didn't reply. He
crouched down next to the barrels.
One was on its side, and a glass tube
stuck out of the top, running across
the deck, all the way to the main
mast. Purple smoke billowed along
inside the tube, clouding around
the base of the mast and working
its way into the wood, giving it a

pulsing, magical sheen.

"Wow," breathed Elenna. "Do you think this is what's powering the ship?"

Tom nodded. "It looks like one of Kensa's potions."

"Are you thinking what I'm thinking?" asked Elenna.

Their gaze met, and they both spoke the same word: "Sabotage!"

Tom whipped out his sword and slashed at the barrels, hacking into them. Smoke spilled out, making him cough and splutter, but he kept going, filling the hold with purple fumes. Elenna stamped on the glass tube, smashing it with her boot and releasing more wisps of smoke.

"Now what?" she said. "It doesn't seem to have—"

The ship's timbers gave a sudden creaking yawn. The deck jolted,

sending Tom and Elenna staggering.
Up above, they heard a thump and
an angry growl from Sanpao.

*He must have fallen out of his
hammock,* thought Tom, with a grin.
"I think it's working!" he shouted.
He kicked another barrel, shattering
it into pieces.

The ship lurched again. This time
Tom felt a sudden weightlessness
in his stomach, and then the vessel
began to tip, diving downwards –
slowly at first, but gaining speed.

Elenna cast a glance at Tom.
"Maybe we should get out of
here now?"

Before Tom could reply, there was
a clatter of footsteps and lantern

light shone from the far end of the hold. He whirled around to see a crowd of Sanpao's pirates approaching, snarling with fury, their cutlasses glinting.

"Like you said," muttered Elenna, drawing her bow. "This was never going to be easy!"

Tom threw himself forwards, swinging his sword. It glanced off a pirate's blade, distracting the thug long enough for Tom to trip him with a swipe of his leg, then jump over his fallen body. He steadied himself as the deck tipped again. Throwing a quick glance over his shoulder, he saw Elenna launching arrows one after another, pinning a pirate's shirt to the mainmast and sending two of his friends scrambling for cover.

An angry roar drew Tom's attention, and he saw another pirate charging at him. It was the woman with the gold earrings, brandishing a huge double-headed axe. Tom ducked as she swung it, letting the weight of the blow throw her off balance. She toppled over his body, sprawling onto a heap of gunpowder sacks.

"Come on!" Tom shouted to Elenna, as the pirate tried to stand. "We've got to find Sanpao!"

He dodged a whirling mace and darted for the steps that led to the

top deck, half running, half sliding, with Elenna hot on his heels.

As they came out into open air, Tom saw that the sails were flapping against the mast. Pirates raced in all directions, desperately lashing down

barrels and pulling on ropes to try
to stop the ship from plummeting.
It was no good, though. Tom and
Elenna grabbed hold of the gunwale
as the ship juddered yet again. A
crate smashed open, scattering fresh

mangoes across the deck. Angel let out a whinny of distress, and Star tossed her head nervously.

Tom leaned over the edge of the ship, and saw with a shock that the fields of Gwildor were gone. Instead, his vision was filled with a vast expanse of glowing red light, pulsing and crackling like an angry ocean. Tom had never seen anything like it.

"Brace yourselves, mates!" roared the pirate captain, from the upper deck. "We're in for a bumpy ride!"

Peering through the shifting red light, Tom recognised the shape of the city of Jengtor far below, spread out like a four-pointed star.

"It's Irina's dome," shouted Elenna suddenly. "The magical one she conjured up to protect the city."

"I think you're right," murmured Tom. *And we're heading straight for it...*

THE ROYAL MUTT

"We have to get to the wheel," said Elenna. "Then maybe we can steer the ship clear of the dome."

"Leave it to me," Tom told her. He sprinted off across the deck, dodging rolling barrels and pirates. Sanpao's crew were far too busy panicking and clinging on to the rigging to stop him.

Tom bounded up the steps to the

stern, then paused to check on Elenna. She was with Angel and Star, stroking their necks and murmuring softly to keep them from bolting. She caught his eye and mouthed two words: *Good luck*.

Taking a deep breath, Tom grabbed hold of the wheel, straining every muscle in his body to turn it.

But it wouldn't budge.

Tom drew on the strength of his golden breastplate, but even with magic flooding through his limbs, he couldn't move it at all. It was jammed.

That's it – we're finished... Glancing up, Tom could see nothing beyond the ship but the vast, curving red surface of Irina's dome. *Will it be a quick death?* he wondered.

Then a second pair of hands clamped onto the wheel. Tom turned to see Sanpao looming over him, eyes wild with fury, but his cutlass safely thrust through his belt.

"I'll kill you later, boy," growled the pirate. "I can promise you that."

"Do your worst," Tom replied. "But right now – help me push!"

They heaved with everything they had, grunting at the effort. Finally the wheel gave way, creaking to the right. The whole crew slid to the side of the deck, as the ship swerved.

"Harder!" roared Sanpao.

Tom rearranged his grip, tensing
his muscles until they ached.
Gritting his teeth, he and Sanpao
forced the wheel round again, and
the ship kept turning.

Tom glanced up ahead and saw

a gaping hole in the red light, the edges of it dull and purple, like a bruise. *That must be the hole Kensa made with her spells!* he realised. And slowly but surely, the ship was veering towards it.

They were too close to avoid the dome now. Their only hope was to squeeze through the gap in one piece. A blood-red shadow fell across the deck. Tom hardly dared watch as they plunged down...

CRACK!

His heart lurched at the noise, until he saw that it was only the ship's figurehead. It had struck the edge of the hole and broken off, tumbling away in a shower of splinters.

We made it!

But there was no time to celebrate. The vessel dipped again, and the city of Jengtor filled Tom's vision, the sprawl of buildings rushing towards them at sickening speed.

"Come on!"Tom shouted at the pirate captain. "We have to—"

Sanpao's fist slammed into his stomach, knocking the air out of him. He fell backwards and knocked his head against the gunwale. Pain burst through his skull. Dazed, he sat up to see the pirate captain take charge of the wheel, his brow furrowed with determination.

They were falling faster and

faster. Buildings rose around them and someone screamed from the streets below.

"We're going to crash!" bellowed Sanpao.

THUNK!

Tom flew up in the air and landed in a heap, his bones jolting with the impact. *We've hit the ground,* he realised, but before he could get to his feet the ship bounced again, and Tom slammed into the deck a second time, face first.

The ship skidded along the ground with a screeching, rumbling roar so loud it made Tom want to cover his ears and curl up in a ball. He lay flat, his body throbbing with pain, bracing himself for the next impact.

CRRRRASH!

He was flung across the deck, and slammed into something.

Tom risked a quick glance upwards and saw chunks of stone falling from overhead, smashing

holes in the deck like rocks hurled
by catapults. *We must have broken
through some kind of wall...*

At long last the thunder of the
timbers died away, and the ship
ground to a halt with one final
ear-splitting squeal of wood and

metal on stone. After that there was nothing but an eerie silence.

Tom's whole body was aching as he cautiously raised his head. He saw the walls of the Emperor Jeng's palace all around them – they had landed in the courtyard. *We must be right in the heart of Jengtor!*

Tom heaved himself up to the railings at the front of the poop deck, scouring the ship for any sign of Elenna. Everywhere pirates were groggily rising to their feet, shaking their heads and nursing injuries. At last Tom spotted his friend, wrestling with the reins of Angel and Star, who were both trembling with fear. Relief flooded through his veins.

"Tom!" yelled Elenna suddenly. "Look out!"

Tom turned to see Sanpao's boot flying at his chest. He dodged just in time, but tripped and went sailing over the side of the ship, stumbling and collapsing on the stone paving of the courtyard. He lay there, motionless, fighting to get his breath back.

Sanpao leapt over the gunwale, landing in a crouch nearby. Tom rolled over, ready to fight, but the pirate wasn't looking at him. Instead his attention was fixed on two figures who were striding out from the main building of the palace.

Tom recognised one straight away.

The tall woman in flowing robes was Kensa, his old enemy and Sanpao's ally – the witch who had poisoned his mother and taken her prisoner.

The second figure shuffled forward, hunched over, dressed in a tatty robe with the hood pulled up so that Tom couldn't see a face. Suddenly he remembered the words of the pirate earlier – *We got an ally in Jengtor.* Someone on the inside. Could it be this strange hooded figure?

Kensa was clapping as she approached, but she didn't look happy.

"Bravo," she sneered. "Quite an entrance, even for you, dear Captain Sanpao. It's a good thing we won't be needing that heap of junk for a getaway." She eyed the wreckage of the pirate ship disdainfully.

"You should have made the hole

bigger," snapped Sanpao, squaring up to her. "And watch what you say about my ship. It'll take days to patch her up, and you know she's the most important lady in my life. She never let me down before."

As his enemies glared at each other, Tom mustered his strength and rose. His mother was inside the palace, and he'd do whatever it took to get her to safety. He started forwards, dashing past Kensa and Sanpao before they had a chance to react. But the hunched, hooded figure stepped into his path.

"Let me past," yelled Tom, drawing his sword.

The figure just let out a harsh laugh.

"You dare to give me orders in my own palace, boy?"

Tom slid to a halt, stunned, as the man threw off his hood and drew himself up to his full, imposing height. He had a shaven head and a proud gaze, and Tom knew at once who he was. He'd seen him in paintings, back in King Hugo's palace in Avantia.

Emperor Jeng!

"Meet our newest ally." Kensa smirked.

Tom could hardly believe it. The emperor himself – ruler of all Gwildor – had betrayed his own people and joined forces with Kensa and Sanpao. *No wonder they're so confident they can take over the kingdom!*

He tried to dodge past, but Jeng was too quick. In one swift movement the emperor had drawn a curved sword from inside his cloak

and sent it flickering at Tom. *Clang!* Tom met it with his own blade. As steel rested on steel, he sensed the strength in the emperor's arm.

Sanpao's pirates were clambering down from the ship, but they kept their distance. Tom caught sight of Elenna on the deck above, peering down at him anxiously. She began to draw her bow, but Tom shook his head. With any luck, he wouldn't need it.

Besides, if she misses, I'll be right in the firing line...

Ruff!

The noise was so unexpected it took Tom a moment to realise what it was.

A dog's bark.

The creature came bounding from

the gates of the palace – a scrawny
black mongrel with a red silk collar.

"Back inside," Emperor Jeng said
roughly. But instead the dog sat,
wagging its tail hopefully.

"The palace mutt," said Kensa,
her voice dripping with distaste.
"Personally I've never understood
what people see in such pathetic
creatures." A slow smile spread
across her face, and she turned to the
Emperor. "But perhaps it might have
its uses...?"

Jeng smirked and nodded. Kensa
reached down, grabbed the dog by
its collar and brought out a vial of
potion from within her cloak. Tom's
heart stopped at the sight of it. It

was the very same potion Kensa had used to create her Evil Beasts, Styro, Ronak and Solix.

"No!" Tom shouted. But it was too late. Kensa emptied the vial onto the dog's back, and foul green fumes drifted into the air.

The creature whimpered, shook itself and spun in a circle, trying to lick itself clean. But there was no way it could reach the potion. The pirates began to mutter and back away nervously.

Tom watched in horror as the dog's skin stretched and expanded, its fur growing out in wild clumps. Its claws lengthened, becoming sharper and more savage. Its collar snapped and dropped to the ground. The dog was growing, whining with the shock of the transformation. Soon it was twice as big, then five times – then ten, its body bulking with muscle...

It loomed over them, sweeping its gaze around the courtyard and sniffing hungrily. Its thick, matted fur gave off a pungent stench, and at the sight of its eyes, Tom caught his breath. They were black and glittering, like shimmering shards of midnight.

Jeng laughed as Kensa clapped her hands together with glee, and a nervous cheer rose from the pirate crew.

Through the red jewel set in his belt,

Tom heard the Beast speak, his voice little more than a snarl.

Greetings, Tom. I am Kanis, the Shadow Hound. *Now face your doom...*

EMPEROR OF AVANTIA

Kanis prowled forward, his thick drool spattering the paving stones. Tom locked eyes with the Beast. He shrugged his shield from his back and raised it, bracing himself for the first attack.

"Five gold coins on the hound!" shouted a pirate.

"Only a fool would bet on the boy," called another. "He'll be dog food in less than a minute!"

"Stow it, mates," growled Sanpao. "We've got a city to plunder!"

The pirates roared their approval. Led by their captain, they rushed out of the courtyard, leaving Tom to his fate.

Tom saw the hackles rise all along the Beast's back, and Kanis's lips raised in a snarl that revealed savage yellow teeth, each one as long as his sword. He backed away, mind racing. There had to be some way to beat this creature... But right now, he was out of ideas.

From the corner of his eye, Tom

saw Elenna leap from the ship and land in the courtyard. She raced over to him.

"What now?" she asked, her gaze fixed on the monstrous creature stalking towards them.

"I'll deal with Kanis," said Tom, trying to sound confident. "You go and warn the people of Jengtor about Sanpao and his crew. Those pirates aren't going to show them any mercy."

Elenna nodded grimly. "Don't worry – I'll stop them. If I can get out of the palace, that is." She threw a glance at Kensa and Emperor Jeng. Tom noticed that both of them seemed mesmerised by the awesome spectacle of the Beast.

Kanis lunged forward, growling
fiercely. Tom darted to one side,
swinging the flat of his blade as

hard as he could. It struck the Beast's nose with a dull thump, but Kanis didn't even seem to feel it.

The dog snapped again. Tom stumbled to get away, but he tripped on a chunk of masonry and fell to his knees. Kanis padded closer, throwing a shadow over him...

Whhhhhsh! An arrow split the air between them, startling the Beast.

Thanks, Elenna.

The Shadow Hound withdrew, sniffing, as though trying to work out what had happened. Elenna nodded at Tom, slung her bow over her shoulder and ran back to the ship.

Tom used his sword to push

himself upright. But before he could attack, something hard struck the back of his knees and sent him sprawling again. He looked up to see Kensa smiling nastily, her knuckles white around her metal staff. Beyond her, Kanis let out one last growl then turned, tail lashing like a serpent, and ran through the open doors back into the main palace building.

Where's it going? Why isn't it staying to finish me off?

Elenna had already led Star down from the wreckage of the ship and was clambering up into the saddle. She threw Tom one last anxious glance.

"Don't worry about me!"Tom shouted at her. "Just warn the citizens!"

His friend hesitated for a moment before kicking her heels and galloping off, out of the main gates and into the city.

Tom turned back to the enemies standing over him. Both Kensa and Jeng were sneering down at him now, as though he were a cockroach they were about to stamp on.

"So this is the famous Tom?" said Jeng. "A snivelling child... I thought he was supposed to be a hero!"

"And I thought you were supposed to be an emperor!"Tom shot back. "What kind of ruler turns on their own people?"

"An ambitious one," replied Jeng.

"What more could you possibly want?" said Tom. "You're the Emperor of Gwildor!"

Jeng just laughed. "Such a simple boy. There is always more. True, I am the Emperor of Gwildor. But one day I shall be Emperor of Avantia too. And then Emperor of all the kingdoms!"

"I don't think so," said Tom. "Not when your allies are a greedy pirate and a mad old witch!"

Kensa's face twisted with rage. "Brave words for a boy in your position," she spat. "A boy who failed to save his own mother. Kanis is hunting for her right now. I'm only sorry she isn't here to see me kill her son…"

Kensa swung her staff at Tom's head. He threw up his shield, and the blow bounced off it with a thud that sent tremors down his arm. He peered over the edge of the shield and saw Emperor Jeng raising a boot to stamp down on his stomach…

Tom tensed his legs against a cracked paving stone and pushed, sliding along the ground on his back. Then he rolled, clambered to his feet and raced away.

"Angel!" he shouted. "Where are you?" The horse appeared at the gunwale of Sanpao's wrecked ship. "Here, girl!" Tom called. Angel leapt from the deck, neighing in fright as she landed in between Tom and his enemies.

"That animal won't save you, child," said Emperor Jeng, swinging his sword in a glittering arc as he approached.

Tom grabbed Angel's saddle and hauled himself up onto it. "Go!" he hissed into the horse's ear, nudging his heels into her flanks. Angel launched herself forwards, charging across the courtyard as Tom clutched onto the reins.

"Stop him!" screeched Kensa.

But the pirates were all gone, and

Jeng just stood there, staring in shock.

Tom flicked the reins, steering Angel towards the main building.

I've got to catch Kanis, and fast. If that Beast finds my mother...

He ducked as Angel galloped in through the doorway. Then he tugged on the reins and scanned around, panting hard. They were in a vast hallway of white stone, with light filtering through glass panes high above. The air was cool and still. Several corridors led off the hallway, and Kanis could have gone down any one of them.

Tom drew on the power of the red jewel, reaching out with his mind, trying to sense if Kanis was nearby.

Suddenly Angel let out a terrified neigh and reared up, almost throwing him onto the floor. Tom caught hold of the reins. His heart stopped. A dark shape was slinking out of the

shadows to their left.

Why didn't I see that before?

The creature shimmered like a mirage, then took on a horribly familiar shape – a vast, powerful hound with glittering black eyes...

Kanis pounced, slamming into Tom and Angel with all the force of an avalanche. Tom went tumbling to the ground, and pain coursed through his leg as Angel fell with him, trapping him beneath her body.

A single thought raced through Tom's mind. *That's why he called himself the Shadow Hound... Because he can actually turn into a shadow!* And then the Beast was snarling over them, teeth bared and dripping with saliva.

Tom kicked desperately with his free leg, hitting Kanis square on the nose. The Beast took a step backwards, shaking his head. Angel writhed upright, and Tom scrambled away.

Rearing up on her hind legs, Angel bravely kicked at the dog's flanks. But her hooves simply bounced off Kanis's fur as though she were kicking solid rock.

His fur is as tough as armour, thought Tom.

Angel kicked Kanis again, and the Shadow Hound turned on her, snarling viciously.

Tom knew he might not get another chance. He swung his blade as hard as he could, aiming for the Beast's leg closest to him. The thud of the impact juddered along his arm, but he was rewarded with a howl. He whipped his sword away and swung it again in a great circle, aiming for Kanis's muzzle this time. *Thunk!* The Beast howled again, tailing off into a whine.

If I can just keep this up...

But when Tom slashed a third time, the blade bit nothing but thin air. Kanis was gone, melting away into his shadow form and flitting away like a dark ghost.

Tom could almost feel his heart sinking.

This battle isn't over. Not by a long shot...

5

FIGHTING SHADOWS

The black shape of Kanis darted down a corridor, heading deeper into the palace. Tom leapt after him, with Angel's hooves echoing on the stone floor as she followed.

I'm coming for you, Mother! I won't let that Beast hurt you...

Tom reached the entrance to

the corridor just in time to see the Shadow Hound disappearing around the corner. Quickly he drew on the power of the golden boots, surging forward with magical speed, so fast that behind him, Angel had to break into a gallop to keep up.

The shadowy form of Kanis sped up too, as though he could sense Tom gaining on him. But at the end of the corridor was a solid stone wall.

A dead end! thought Tom. He pushed himself harder, charging after Kanis. *Now he'll have to face me...*

Tom flinched as the Beast struck the wall. But instead of there being

a thunderous crash, the Shadow
Hound simply slipped right through
the stone, as though it weren't there
at all. He was gone.

Tom skidded to a halt, his mind racing.

No way through. Unless...

An idea came to him – the white jewel in his belt gave him the power to separate his shadow from his body. So even if his body couldn't pass through the wall, his shadow might be able to.

He reached for his belt, his fingers pressing on the white jewel that was set into it. He felt it pulse with magic, and his mind seemed to shimmer, as part of him split away. He concentrated hard, taking a step forward and looking down at the dark, ghostly form of his own shadow. Looking back, he saw his body standing still, eyes blank.

Beyond, Angel let out a whinny of confusion and tossed her head.

Tom felt a surge of triumph. With the power of the jewel, he had taken control of his shadow, splitting it from his body.

He forced it to move, leaving himself behind. The shadow stepped through the wall after Kanis, and into an empty banqueting hall.

Tom's shadow flitted forward, moving right through tables and chairs as it crossed the hall. A dark tapestry shifted and Tom saw that the Beast had been lying in wait against it. Kanis prowled forward, a shimmering black nightmare.

Lucky I'm a shadow myself,
thought Tom. *There's no way it can
hurt me!*

But no sooner had he thought
it than the Beast swiped at his
shadow with a paw, and Tom felt it
connect, hard and heavy. The blow
bowled his shadow to the ground
and left him throbbing with pain.
He tried to clamber upright but the
Beast pounced again, pinning his
shadow down, paws weighing on
his shoulders.

Tom concentrated as hard as he
could, trying to control his shadow.
It squirmed free and spun round,
swinging its shadow blade at
Kanis.

*Maybe if the Beast can strike
my shadow, my shadow can strike
him back...*

But Kanis had already backed out
of reach. His dark shape flickered

and turned solid again, and before Tom's shadow could dodge, the Beast twisted his head, snapping his jaws shut around it.

CLACK! The Beast's teeth met as they passed straight through.

Even in shadow form, Tom felt relief flood through him.

So we can only fight each other when we're both real – or both shadows!

Kanis must have worked this out too, because the next moment the hound flickered again, turning back into a shadow and surging forward.

Tom sent his own shadow somersaulting backwards, out of reach. But as it landed, he saw that

Kanis hadn't slowed down. Instead the Beast raced on, charging through the wall.

Tom followed. And as his shadow passed through the stone, he felt a nauseous tug at his insides.

They were in a much smaller chamber, where the walls were lined with shelf upon shelf of dusty old books, and a battered old desk stood cluttered with vials of potions. On a bench at the far wall lay a figure Tom would have recognised anywhere.

Mother!

Freya's eyes were closed. She was breathing peacefully, seeming totally unaware of what was going

on around her. At her side stood a
woman with long, dark hair, her
blue cloak speckled with stars – the
Good Witch, Irina.

The witch's eyes were open wide and her hands were tightly clasped around the hilt of Freya's sword. The blade wavered as she held it out, pointing it at the Shadow Hound. "Get away from us!" she hissed.

But instead Kanis stalked towards them, licking his lips...

6

ANT ARMOUR

There's no way I can stop that Beast, thought Tom. *Not without my body!*

With the power of the white jewel, he sent his shadow darting back, straight through the banqueting hall. A shudder ran through him, as he became himself once more.

No time to lose. With every

passing moment, his mother and Irina were in greater danger.

"Wait here!" Tom told Angel. Then he raced off down the passageway, taking a left turn, then another, trying to find his way back to Irina's chamber. Rounding another corner he reached a narrow wooden door, and skidded to a halt. *This has to be it...* He pressed his ear against the wood, and sure enough, the voice of Irina came from inside, trembling with fear.

"Leave us alone! Please..."

Tom twisted the iron ring of the door handle, but it wouldn't budge.

They must have barricaded themselves in!

A low growl sounded from the chamber, making the entire door vibrate.

Tom took five paces back and concentrated hard, drawing on the power of his golden breastplate. Then he called on the power of his golden chainmail, and on his golden leg armour. His body hummed with magical strength.

"Here goes," he murmured. Then he launched himself forward, charging as fast as he could.

Crrrrrassh! He barged into the door, tearing it from its hinges and cracking it in two. Stumbling into the room, he almost tripped over the fallen scraps of wood.

At once he saw the Shadow Hound crouched over Irina and Freya, jaws slavering.

Just in time, boy, growled the voice of the Beast. *Now watch me tear your mother limb from limb...*

Tom's shoulder throbbed with pain where it had hit the door. Lunging at Kanis, he let his momentum carry him as he dived underneath the Beast. He twisted and saw the dog's soft underbelly, where the fur was paler and thinner. Landing on his back, he hacked his sword upwards.

Kanis reared up, letting out a fearsome growl.

Irina flung her hand out, and a ball of bright red light streaked towards

the Beast, smacking Kanis in his
underbelly for a second time and
sending him writhing away.

As Tom leapt to his feet, Kanis

swiped a paw at Irina, pinning her to the wall. The Beast's tail lashed out, catching Tom a stinging blow across the face. He staggered to the ground once again, dropping his sword and shield with a clatter on the stone floor.

Through the doorway, Tom saw that Angel had followed him, and was waiting there nervously. She gave a whinny, and tossed her mane. Tom couldn't blame her.

Kanis is practically unbeatable! He's far stronger than me, and his fur is as tough as steel.

Wait...

Tom became very aware of the ant armour gloves beneath his tunic.

He had stuffed them there after his battle with Solix and, in all the chaos that followed, had forgotten about them until now.

Maybe I can use them to wrestle Kanis into submission!

"Help me!" gasped Irina.

Tom rummaged inside his tunic, finding the gloves and tugging them on as fast as he could. They were rigid, sticky and uncomfortable, but that didn't matter. He turned and raced back into the chamber.

"Come and get me, Kanis!" he shouted.

The Beast turned from Irina, letting her drop weakly to the ground. His lips curled in a snarl as he prowled towards Tom, hackles bristling, claws clicking on the floor.

Tom's heart was thumping. *This had better work...*

He darted in, reaching for the Beast's jaws. Kanis jerked away, unsure what was happening. But it was too late – the gloves closed around the hound's head.

Kanis writhed, rattling Tom's body like a bag of bones and sending shards of pain through his aching shoulder. But the gloves held fast, sticking tight to the fur.

It must be Solix's magic, thought Tom. *I'm using Kensa's own Beasts against each other!*

The Shadow Hound flicked his

head angrily, lifting Tom off his feet.

Tom's stomach lurched with fear,
but he tensed his muscles, using
the momentum to swing into a
somersault and landing face up on
the Beast's back. Pulling the gloves

free, he twisted round, staying as low as he could. He pressed his knees into the dog's flanks, gripping Kanis's head again with the gloves, more firmly this time.

Peering down at the thick fur on Kanis's neck, Tom saw where the black was stained purple from Kensa's foul potion. He wrinkled his nose at the stench.

The Beast's body rumbled with another growl. He shook himself fiercely, and it was all Tom could do to cling on.

What now?

If only he had his sword...

"Tom!"

He cast a quick glance over the

Beast's shoulders. Irina had picked
up his sword, and was waving it
at him.

"Catch!" shouted the witch, and
she threw it. The sword glinted as it
spun through the air...

Tom tugged his right hand free

and reached for the hilt. At the
same moment Kanis reared up, and
Tom had to squeeze his knees in
even tighter to stop himself sliding
off the Beast's back. He caught the
sword, almost tipping over as he

stretched for it. And as Kanis fell
down onto his forepaws again, Tom
swiped his blade at the discoloured
hair on the Beast's neck.

Whsshh!

The hairs came free in a spray of

purple, drifting slowly downwards.

Kanis let out an anguished howl, so loud it froze Tom's blood. The Shadow Hound writhed, and this time Tom couldn't keep his balance. He went tumbling head over heels, smacking into the stone floor and crumpling in a heap against a wall.

But as he raised his head, he saw that something incredible was happening. Kanis was shrinking. His claws were retracting, his muscles disappearing and his growl getting softer, until it was little more than a whimper.

Within seconds, Kensa's foul Beast was no more, and Emperor Jeng's pet dog sat in its place, panting, its pink tongue hanging out. It trotted over to Tom, sniffed at his shoes and rolled on its back.

Tom met Irina's gaze, and the witch smiled.

"I think Kanis wants a belly rub," said Irina.

7

THE POISONED FANG

Tom leapt to his feet and crossed the chamber, kneeling at his mother's side. She was still deathly pale and her eyes were tightly closed.

"Is she going to be all right?" Tom asked.

Irina's smile dropped at once. "I'm sorry, Tom," said the witch, gently.

"She's still alive, but I have nothing to cure her with."

Irina turned over Freya's arm and on the underside Tom saw that the veins were raised and flowing with a green fluid.

"Can't you make an antidote?" said Tom, desperately. "There must be something you can do."

Irina shrugged. "Perhaps if I knew the poison..."

A dog's bark cut her off. Tom turned to see that Kanis had trotted forward, and was nudging at something on the ground with his nose – something long, and white as bone. The dog barked again.

A tooth!

Peering closer, Tom saw that the dog was missing one of its own two canine teeth.

So the fang is all that remains of

*the Shadow Hound. A Beast created
by Kensa's evil potion.*

As Tom bent to pick up the tooth,
he saw that the tip was glistening
blue. He showed it to Irina. "What
does it mean?" he asked.

Irina frowned. "I have read that
it's possible for poisons to cancel
each other out," she said. "Or…" Her
gaze met Tom's, and he saw that she
was thinking the same as him.

"Or…it could kill her," Tom
whispered. But what choice did
they have?

Irina nodded towards Freya's arm.
"This is for you to do, Tom," she said
quietly. "Pierce the vein. With luck,
Kensa's poisons will destroy each

other. We can only hope."

Tom nodded and clenched the fang tight, like a dagger. Behind him, Kanis let out a soft whine, and Angel whinnied. It was as though they both realised.

Freya's life depends on this.

Tom took a deep breath and pushed the tooth into his mother's arm. A thick bead of greenish blood

sprang up and dripped to the floor. Irina pressed a bandage to the wound, and gently pulled the tooth free.

"What now?" murmured Tom.

"Now we must wait," replied Irina.

Tom could feel his heart pounding like a war-drum. Silence. Freya didn't move – not even a flutter of an eyelash.

It's over, thought Tom. I've probably only made it worse. And now my mother's going to die, all because of me. His chest tightened, and he swallowed hard.

"Wait!" gasped Irina.

Tom stared at his mother's arm. The greenish tinge in her veins was

growing paler. He looked to her
face, and saw the pink returning
to her cheeks. Her lips quivered,
and her chest rose and fell. It was
only when she opened her eyes that

Tom realised he'd been holding his breath, and let it out in a great sigh of relief.

"Tom," said Freya, her voice a dry croak. "What in all of Gwildor are you doing here?"

Tom threw his arms around her and hugged her tight.

"I'll explain, Mother, I promise," he said, when he'd managed to stop grinning. "But first, the kingdom needs its Mistress of the Beasts."

Tom hurried through the palace courtyard with Freya at his side. He couldn't believe how quickly she'd recovered. Her eyes glinted with purpose, and Tom could tell she was just as determined as he was. Irina had stayed behind in her chamber, promising to take care of Angel.

Kensa and Jeng were nowhere to be seen as Tom and his mother picked their way over the rubble of the wall smashed down by the pirate ship. The street outside was empty, but a swell of angry shouting carried to their ears. They broke into a run, following the sounds.

In a large square they found Sanpao's crew, crowded around a statue of the emperor in the centre, clutching their weapons tightly, looking wary and anxious. A mob of citizens had the pirates surrounded.

The citizens were armed with
flaming torches, makeshift spears,
knives and axes. Tom's heart leapt

as he saw Elenna among them, an arrow nocked on her bowstring.

"Give up, Sanpao!" shouted Elenna. "You're outnumbered."

The pirate captain jostled his way to the front of his crew. "Aye, that may be so, little girl," he snarled. "But my men are fighters, and yours are shopkeepers. *You* give up!"

"I don't think so!" Elenna shot back.

Tom heard his mother gasp beside him, and saw her pointing at something. Right at the back of the pirate crew, skulking close by his own statue, was Emperor Jeng. His eyes darted left and right, as though nervous that his people would spot him. Kensa was at his side, waiting to see what would happen next.

"So the emperor is a traitor?" muttered Freya.

Tom nodded. "He's been on Kensa's side, all along."

Freya's eyes narrowed and her brow creased in thought. "Wait – I remember now," she said. "Before I fell ill, there was a banquet, and Jeng poured wine for me. I thought it was strange at the time – normally that's a servant's job."

"He must have poisoned you himself!" Tom felt his cheeks burning with anger. "Well, he won't get away with it."

But just as Tom was about to

charge in, Captain Sanpao let out a roar of anger, drew his cutlass and leapt forward – straight at Elenna.

GUARDIANS OF GWILDOR

The pirates raised a ragged battle cry and rushed at the citizens. "Raaaaaaah!"

Tom darted at Sanpao, sword raised. He saw Elenna let fly with an arrow, forcing the pirate captain to dodge, but the next moment Sanpao was swept away by a surge

of citizens, and Tom found himself
confronted by a heavy-looking
pirate wielding an iron mace.

Tom parried, kicking the pirate
in the stomach and sending him
reeling. Another came at him, twin

swords flailing. Tom ducked and weaved away. Steel clashed all around him, as he tried to find a clear space to see what was going on. Jumping up on a wooden crate he saw his mother wading in, laying about her with a wooden staff in one hand and a sword in the other. The citizens were fighting bravely, holding off the pirates, while Elenna loosed arrow after arrow at Sanpao's crew.

We're winning!

Then Tom caught sight of a pair of figures prowling on the other side of the square. Emperor Jeng and Kensa had slipped away from the statue and were watching the battle.

Tom's heart raced. If Kensa started using magic against them, they were in serious trouble. He couldn't bear the thought of any more citizens losing their lives to the Evil Witch...

"Don't worry, Tom!" called a familiar voice.

He looked up to see his mother smiling at him, resting the end of her staff on an unconscious pirate. She nodded at Kensa, as though she had guessed what he was thinking. "I don't think she's going to cause us any more problems."

Tom frowned. "How can you be so sure?"

Before his mother could reply, a deep tremor ran through the ground, throwing several fighters off balance and making even the buildings around the square shudder in their foundations.

An earthquake? thought Tom. But then the ground shook again, and again. *No – not an earthquake...*

Footsteps!

Tom looked up to see a gigantic figure looming over the city, casting them all in shadow. The creature was made of red stone – half man, half mountain. Tom's heart leapt.

It's Rokk! One of the Good Beasts of Gwildor...

The Walking Mountain ground a fist into his palm with a sound like an avalanche.

"What is that?" screeched a
pirate. Sanpao's crew were gazing
upwards, wide-eyed in horror. A

few broke and ran for the nearest
alleyway leading off the square,
but they came skidding to a halt as
another creature swooped from the
sky, a great bird which landed in the
alley and folded its golden wings,
strutting forward, hissing with
menace.

Hawkite!

Tom caught his mother's eye,
and matched her grin with one of
his own.

*She's called on the Good Beasts of
Gwildor to save the kingdom!*

The pirates scattered, dropping
their weapons and racing in all
directions. Above the rooftops Tom
caught a glimpse of another huge

figure approaching the square, this one made of glittering ice. A buzzing green insect Beast hovered low from the opposite direction, pincers clicking. *Koldo and Amictus. But where's Trema?*

As if in answer to his question, the ground erupted nearby, and a

blue armoured head burst out, jaws snapping, clawed arms snatching at pirates.

The citizens of Jengtor stood gaping at the sight of the Beasts wreaking havoc among the pirates.

"Come on!" Tom shouted. "Let's get them!"

He leapt down from the crate as Freya, Elenna and Irina rallied the citizens, hustling them into a circle to surround Sanpao's crew. The pirates threw their weapons to the ground, raising their hands in panic. From the fear etched on their faces, Tom could tell they'd lost all stomach for the fight.

"Look out!" yelled Elenna suddenly.

Tom spun and saw a figure streaking across the square towards him, snarling with fury, his cutlass raised. *Sanpao!* It was all Tom could do to fling up his shield in time. The pirate's blow shuddered through it. Tom swiped his own blade wildly, and felt it slice through something soft.

"Gaaaaah!" the pirate howled.

Peering over the edge of his shield, Tom saw Sanpao staring in horror at something he had clutched in the palm of his hand – a hank of black hair.

I must have cut off his ponytail!

"Years, it took me to grow that," mumbled Sanpao. "Years!"

Tom felt a grin spread across his face. He slashed again, knocking Sanpao's cutlass out of his hand while he was distracted.

The pirate captain sank to his knees, head hung low. He was defeated, at last.

Tom turned to see the citizens and the pirates all watching him in silence.

"The enemies of Gwildor have been vanquished!" he announced.

"Not so fast!" came an angry shout from the edge of the square. Emperor Jeng strode forward, drawing himself up in his ragged robes. "This is my kingdom, remember? I say who our enemies are. And I say we must throw out this invader Tom at once!"

No one moved a muscle.

"I said throw him out!" demanded the emperor.

A burly citizen stepped forward, face to face with Jeng. "You

betrayed us all," said the citizen.
"You let pirates loose in the city."
Murmurs of agreement came from
his companions. "If anyone's going
to be thrown out, it should be you!"

The citizens fanned out, forming a circle around Jeng and Kensa. A chant rose up, just one or two voices at first, then more, until everyone had joined in. "Down with Jeng! Down with Jeng!"

"Worthless traitors!" howled Emperor Jeng, as the citizens closed in.

But before they could reach him, Kensa stepped into their path, smiling. She drew a vial from inside her robes and tossed it to the ground, where it smashed, and a cloud of thick red smoke billowed out.

The citizens stumbled to a halt, confused and frightened. Within seconds, the smoke had hidden Kensa and Jeng entirely from view. And when it cleared, the witch and the emperor were nowhere to be seen.

"Kensa?" whimpered Sanpao. "You can't just leave me here."

But there was no reply. Kensa was gone.

Tom clenched his fists. *I can't believe she got away again!*

Freya approached, throwing her arms wide and scooping him up into a big hug. "Don't worry, Tom," she whispered. "You saved the people of Gwildor – that's the important thing. Thank goodness you were here for them!"

"It was you who saved the city, Mother!" said Tom, doing his best to smile. He knew the truth, though. *It's not over.* Gwildor was safe for now. They had rescued his mother, and brought peace back to Jengtor. But something told him they hadn't seen the last of Kensa and Jeng.

He caught sight of Elenna, helping the citizens to march Sanpao and the pirates off to the palace dungeons. She flashed a grin at him, and Tom felt his heart swell with pride.

Whatever happens, Elenna and I are a team. And not even Kensa can stand up to us!

CONGRATULATIONS, YOU HAVE COMPLETED THIS QUEST!

At the end of each chapter you were awarded a special gold coin. The QUEST in this book was worth an amazing 11 coins.

Look at the Beast Quest totem picture inside the back cover of this book to see how far you've come in your journey to become

MASTER OF THE BEASTS.

The more books you read, the more coins you will collect!

Do you want your own
Beast Quest Totem?
1. Cut out and collect the coin below
2. Go to the Beast Quest website
3. Download and print out your totem
4. Add your coin to the totem
www.beastquest.co.uk/totem

Don't miss the next exciting Beast Quest book, YAKORIX THE ICE BEAR!

Read on for a sneak peek...

A WINTER WITH NO SPRING

Tom's icy fingers tingled as he stretched them towards the parlour fire. Outside, the wind was raging. Tom could hear it howling through chinks in the palace mortar as if Luna the Moon Wolf was trying to break in. He glanced towards the window. Leaden clouds were hurling more snow towards the already smothered ground. *Is this storm ever going to stop?* Tom wondered, leaning closer to the blaze. He glanced towards his friends on the bench beside him. Daltec, Avantia's Wizard, was gazing thoughtfully over the rim of his teacup at the flames while Elenna huddled inside her cloak munching a slice of toast. Across from their bench, King Hugo and Queen Aroha were taking their breakfast from a low table before the hearth. Aduro, the former Wizard, sat close to the fire, his eyes half closed and his chin on his chest.

"More tea?" King Hugo asked, turning towards the queen.

Aroha was almost lost inside a pile of thick woollen robes, but her green eyes sparkled. "If it isn't already frozen," she said. She let out a brittle laugh. "You know, Hugo, if I'd had any idea Avantian winters could be like this, I'd never have agreed to the wedding."

"If *I'd* known that Avantian winters could be like this," Hugo said, "I would have insisted we rule from your castle in Tangala."

Aroha smiled. "You'd never leave the people in their time of need," she said. Then she sat upright, her expression suddenly grave. "That reminds me," she said. "Captain Harkman told me this morning that the stockpiles of wood and grain we've been sending out to the villages are running low. If this winter goes on much longer, I don't know—"

The queen broke off as another icy gust swept across the room, making the candle flames dip and waver. Dark shadows reached up the parlour walls like gnarled fingers, and the endless screeching of the wind echoed in Tom's mind like evil laughter.

This terrible winter is bringing Avantia to its knees as surely as any Beast could, he thought. *But I can't fight the wind! Unless...*

Tom frowned, a dark thought taking shape in his mind. He turned to Daltec on the bench beside him. "Daltec?"Tom said. "You've been studying Avantia's weather records. Do you think this cold is natural? Or could there be a more sinister cause?"

Daltec tipped his head in thought, gnawing at his lip. Across the table, the king and queen waited, their faces etched with worry. "It's hard to say," Daltec answered at last. "The palace records do tell of hard winters in the kingdom's distant past. And weather is unpredictable..."

In his seat beside the fire, Aduro

shook his head. "We have seen hard winters before, yes. But never like this. I had been hoping the weather would change, but now –" Aduro glanced at the bleak view through the window – "I fear Tom may be right."

King Hugo's frown deepened. "So you think this weather is the work of one of Avantia's enemies?"

Aduro nodded. "I am starting to believe so, yes."

The queen gave a tired-sounding laugh. "Unfortunately that leaves us with rather a long list," she said. "Avantia has many foes."

Another gust of wind whirled through the chamber, snuffing out the candles and plunging them all into gloom. Tom heard a door bang shut below. He leapt from the bench as footsteps clattered up the stairs outside, accompanied by the sound of muffled voices.

"You need have no fear," Tom heard Captain Harkman say. "I said he'll see you and he'll see you. King Hugo turns no one away." There was a hurried rap at the door, and Captain Harkman entered followed by a man and a woman wrapped in threadbare cloaks. Their faces were pinched with hunger, and red-raw from the wind. As they turned towards the king, Tom noticed their eyes looked haunted and desperate.

"Your Majesty," the man said, bowing his head. "My name is Jerald, and I farm land up to the north in Yotai. Or at least, I used to. Now my fields are as hard as iron, and lie buried under snow. We cannot sow. We cannot farm. People will starve if there is no let-up in this storm."

Read *Yakorix the Ice Bear* to find out what happens next!

FIGHT THE BEASTS,
FEAR THE MAGIC

Are you a BEAST QUEST mega fan?
Do you want to know about all the latest news,
competitions and books before anyone else?

Then join our Quest Club!

Visit the BEAST QUEST website
and sign up today!

www.beastquest.co.uk

Discover the new Beast Quest mobile game from

Available free on iOS and Android

  **amazon**.com

Guide Tom on his Quest to free the Good Beasts
of Avantia from Malvel's evil spells.

 Battle the Beasts, defeat the minions,
unearth the secrets and collect
rewards as you journey through the
Kingdom of Avantia.

DOWNLOAD THE APP TO BEGIN
THE ADVENTURE NOW!